Love from Frank

S0-AFH-869

To my darling Violet,
who is always kind to bugs

Copyright © 1994 by Callaway & Kirk Company LLC.
All rights reserved. Published by Callaway Arts & Entertainment. Callaway and the Callaway logotype, and Callaway Arts & Entertainment are trademarks.
Miss Spider and all related characters are trademarks and/or registered trademarks of Callaway & Kirk Company LLC.

Nicholas Callaway, President and Publisher
Manuela Roosevelt, Editorial Director · Danielle Sweet, Managing Editor
Toshiya Masuda, Art Director · Ivan Wong, Production Manager
Gordon Goff, Consultant · Jake Anderson, Production Management · Usana Shadday, Press Supervision

No part of this publication may be reproduced, stored in a retrieval system, or transmitted in any form
or by any means, electronic, mechanical, photocopying, recording, or otherwise, without written permission of the publisher.

ISBN: 978-0-935112-13-9

Library of Congress Cataloging-in-Publication data available

25 24 23 22   17 18 19

Printed in China

Distributed in the US by Ingram Publisher Services
2018

The paintings in this book are oils on paper.

Miss Spider's Tea Party

paintings and verse by David Kirk

CALLAWAY

New York

2018

ONE lonely spider sipped her tea
While gazing at the sky.
She watched the insects on the leaves,
And many flying by.
"If I had friends like these," she sighed,
"Who'd stay a while with me,
I'd sit them down on silken chairs
And serve them cakes and tea."

Two timid beetles — Ike and May —
Crept from the woodwork that same day.
But when Miss Spider begged, "Please stay?"
They shrieked, "Oh no!" and dashed away.

Three fireflies flew inside that night,
Their spirits high, their tails alight.
They spied the web and squeaked in fear,
"We'd better get away from here!"
The little trio did not feel
They'd care to be a spider's meal.

Four bumblebees buzzed by outside.
"Please come to tea!" Miss Spider cried.
The four ignored her swaying there.
She waved a tea towel in the air.
She took a cup and tapped the glass.
Then one bee spoke to her at last:
"We would be fools to take our tea
With anyone so spidery."

Within the shadows of the room,
Just peeking from behind a broom,
Five grinning faces bobbed and peered.
Miss Spider smiled. Her heart was cheered.
Descending for a closer look,
She danced into the gloomy nook
But sadly found those jolly mugs
Belonged, alas! to rubber bugs.

Some ants strode in, they numbered six,
But ants with spiders will not mix.
She brewed them tea from hips of roses;
The proud platoon turned up their noses.

A fine bouquet concealed its prize
Of seven dainty butterflies.
Miss Spider, watching from the wall,
Was not aware of them at all.

The tea table was set for eight
With saucers, cups, and silver plate.
The cakes were fresh, the service gleamed,
Yet no one would arrive, it seemed.
Her company in no demand
Left her a cup for every hand.

Nine spotted moths kept safe and warm
In shelter from a thunderstorm.
They stood beneath an open sash
And watched the jagged lightning flash.
Miss Spider dropped down on a thread,
A silver tray above her head.
She'd hoped to please them, but instead . . .

They flew away in mortal dread!

"They've left me all alone," she cried.
She dabbed her eyes and sadly sighed.
"It's plain no bug will ever stay."
Her tears splashed down upon the tray.

Ten tiny steaming cups of tea
Were perched atop her trembling knee.
She sipped and sobbed, then heard a cough
And turned to see a small wet moth —
A fragile thing so soaked by rain,
His wings too damp to fly again.

She smiled and took a checkered cloth
To cloak the frail and thankful moth.
They talked and snacked on tea and pie
Until his tiny wings were dry.
Then lifting him with tender care
She tossed him gently in the air.

The moth told Ike, then Ike told May,
Who went from bug to bug to say,
"There is no reason for alarm.
She's never meant us any harm!"
So later on that afternoon,
Assembled in the dining room,
Eleven insects came to tea
To share Miss Spider's courtesy.

Twelve tender violets in a vase
Presented at Miss Spider's place
Set by her chair, so neatly spun.
She munched the blossoms, one by one.
Her friends were glad to watch her feast
Upon the floral centerpiece.
It was a great relief to see
She ate just flowers and drank just tea.
Miss Spider's reputation grew.
Before too long our hostess knew
Each bug who crawled or hopped or flew
And all their lovely children too.

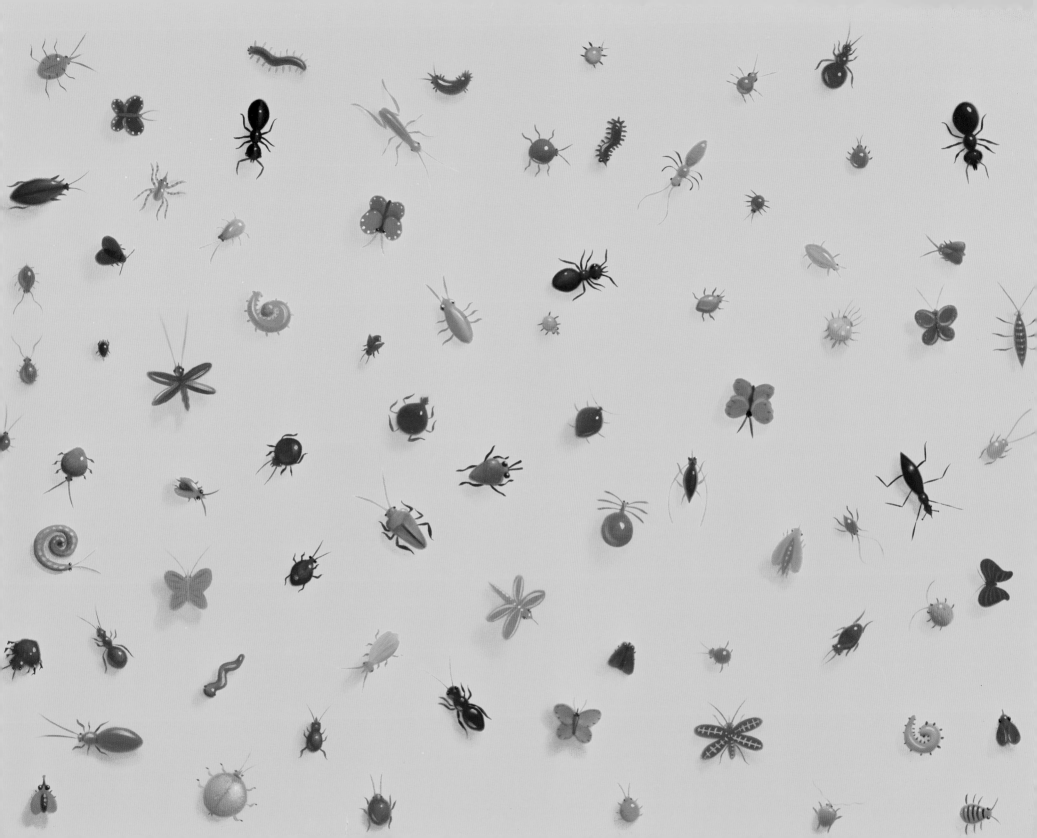